Hush, Puppy

Sigmund Brouwer

illustrated by
Sabrina Gendron

orca Echoes

ORCA BOOK PUBLISHERS

To Hazel—I'm glad you like animals and puns as much as Charlie and Amy do!

Text copyright © Sigmund Brouwer 2022
Illustrations copyright © Sabrina Gendron 2022

Published in Canada and the United States in 2022 by Orca Book Publishers.
orcabook.com

Library and Archives Canada Cataloguing in Publication
Title: Hush, puppy / Sigmund Brouwer ; illustrated by Sabrina Gendron.
Names: Brouwer, Sigmund, 1959- author. | Gendron, Sabrina, illustrator.
Series: Orca echoes.
Description: Series statement: Orca echoes | Charlie's rules ; #3
Identifiers: Canadiana (print) 20210250208 | Canadiana (ebook) 20210250216 |
ISBN 9781459825901 (softcover) | ISBN 9781459810570 (PDF) | ISBN 9781459810587 (EPUB)
Classification: LCC PS8553.R68467 H87 2022 | DDC jc813/.54—dc23

Library of Congress Control Number: 2021941348

Summary: In this partially illustrated early chapter book and the third book in the Charlie's Rules series, eleven-year-old Charlie and his best friend, Amy, rescue a man from a swarm of bees and help an insecure Chihuahua regain his confidence.

Orca Book Publishers is committed to reducing the consumption of nonrenewable resources in the production of our books. We make every effort to use materials that support a sustainable future.

Orca Book Publishers gratefully acknowledges the support for its publishing programs provided by the following agencies: the Government of Canada, the Canada Council for the Arts and the Province of British Columbia through the BC Arts Council and the Book Publishing Tax Credit.

Cover and interior illustrations by Sabrina Gendron
Design by Dahlia Yuen
Edited by Liz Kemp
Author photo by Rebecca Wellman

Printed and bound in Canada.

25   24   23   22 • 1   2   3   4

Chapter One

Charlie Dembinski looked up from the counter as the door opened into the waiting area of the veterinary clinic.

It was Amy Ma. Five minutes late, as usual. Charlie's mother, Selena, was a veterinarian. Amy's mom was the clinic's bookkeeper, and she and Amy lived in the guesthouse on Charlie's family's ranch.

Amy smiled at the only other person in the room—a tall man sitting in the corner, holding a gray cat.

"Hi," she said to the man. "Do you happen to have a dog? I'm starting a new business. Dog walking. I need to earn money for my mom's birthday present."

"Just this cat," he said with a tight, sad smile. He rubbed the cat's head. "I think she has a tumor."

"I'm so sorry to hear that," Amy said. "Dr. Dembinski is the best. You and your cat are in good hands."

She marched over to where Charlie sat behind the counter. The clinic had just opened for the day, and Selena was already in surgery at the back of the building, doing a hip replacement for a German shepherd.

Since it was summer break, Charlie and Amy worked mornings in the clinic, answering the phone and taking questions from anyone who came in with a sick animal. In the afternoons Charlie built doghouses to sell on the clinic's website. Amy's doghouses didn't look quite good enough to sell.

Amy dropped a sheet of paper on the counter and pointed. "What do you think?"

Instead of answering, Charlie stood and walked to the window that overlooked the small parking lot. Beside it was a driveway that led past the vet clinic to the ranch where he lived with his mom and dad and his baby sister. Behind the house were three red barns, and behind that was a long view to faraway hills. Charlie loved living here.

From his spot at the window, he could see the sign at the road.

DEMBINSKI VETERINARY CLINIC
DR. SELENA DEMBINSKI, DVM
(Open weekends)

DVM stood for Doctor of Veterinary Medicine. Charlie was proud of his mom for that. It took a lot of work and dedication to become a veterinarian.

The top half of the sign always stayed the same. It was one of Charlie's jobs to change the letters on the bottom half once per week. With a new animal pun. His mom liked puns. Charlie, not so much.

What he saw now was this: **What do you call 100 rabbits walking backward? A receding hare line!**

For a few more moments, Charlie pretended he was looking for something outside.

"Was it a car or a cat I saw?" he finally said.

"Probably both," Amy answered from the counter. "There's a cat in here,

and this nice man must have driven here in a car."

"Actually," Charlie said, feeling a rare moment of victory, "I just got you with a—"

"Yes, a palindrome" Amy said. "You already got me with it once. You actually thought it would work again?"

Charlie turned and shrugged. "It was worth a try. I thought I'd catch you when you are only half-awake."

"Catch her?" the man with the cat said. "Palindrome?"

"Yes," Charlie answered. "I always get up early. Amy likes to sleep in. Sometimes, if she isn't paying attention, I manage to trick her with one."

The man looked puzzled as he scratched the cat's head. "One what?"

"A palindrome," Charlie said.

"Like my name," Amy said. "Amy Ma. No *h* in Ma. Same as *race car*. Reads the same forward and backward."

Amy flipped over her piece of paper on the counter. She took a pen from her back pocket and quickly wrote on the back of the paper: WAS IT A CAR OR A CAT I SAW.

She held it in front of the man's face. He stared at the sentence. Then he smiled. This time it was a real smile.

"Cool," he said.

"What do you think about my poster?" she asked. She showed him the other side of the piece of paper. "For my new dog-walking business. Dr. Dembinski said I could put this up in the clinic. Should I have a drawing of a dog on this poster?"

"I suppose it wouldn't hurt," the man said.

"That's what I thought. But I'm a bad artist. Maybe Charlie can help."

"I'm not good at art either," Charlie said. He had already returned to the counter to answer the phone if it rang.

"Draw, O coward!" she said.

"I'd wreck your poster," he said. "Sorry."

Amy began to giggle. "Gotcha."

Charlie blinked a few times. Then he groaned. "Was that the whole reason for your poster? Just to get me with that one?"

"No," Amy said. "I really do need to make some money for my mom's birthday present."

"I'm confused," the man said, still petting his cat. "Got him with what?"

Charlie sighed. He found another piece of paper and wrote on it in big block letters: DRAW O COWARD.

He held it above his head. "Palindrome."

The man squinted, then nodded. "Yup, she did get you. Who's winning?"

"You really have to ask?" Amy said. "By the way, why do you think your cat has a tumor?"

"I can feel it when I rub her belly."

He held the cat out to her.

Charlie was getting used to this now. The man wouldn't let him touch the cat. But something about Amy made people feel more comfortable.

"Hmm," she said, rubbing the cat's belly. "I can definitely feel something. I'm wondering if—"

She didn't get a chance to finish. A loud honking car horn interrupted her.

She gave the cat back to the man as Charlie stepped around the counter. They reached the window at the same time.

The honking was coming from the parking lot. An elderly man was behind the steering wheel of a car, honking and honking.

It looked as though the rear window of the car was covered by a huge swarm of bees!

Chapter Two

"Bees?" Amy said.

"Bees!" Charlie said.

"Where?" the man with the cat said. "I'm allergic to bees!"

He moved to the window and shrieked at the sight of the swarm. "Don't let them inside!"

He ran with his cat down the hall to the bathroom and locked himself inside.

"The man driving the car looks terrified," Amy said.

"Mom's in surgery," Charlie said. "Dad's in town. What next? Call the police? Call the fire station?"

"They would take at least fifteen minutes to get here." Amy slapped Charlie on the back. "But thanks for the great idea!"

"Idea?"

"Firefighters use fire extinguishers. It's down the hall, right?"

"Yes, but…"

Too late. Amy had rushed away.

Charlie had a different idea. He held up his hand to the man in the car, to signal that he needed a minute, and rushed back to the computer. He had his fingers on the keyboard when Amy returned.

"Any idea how these things work?" she asked. She held the fire extinguisher in her arms.

"That might not be a good idea," Charlie said. "If you just give me a minute here..."

The honking outside continued.

"A minute? Something needs to be done *now*! That poor man out there needs our help!"

Amy set the fire extinguisher upright on the floor. She knelt beside it.

"Don't worry," she told Charlie. "Instructions are here on the side."

Charlie was focused on the computer screen.

" 'Pull the pin,' " Amy said. "Got it. Then 'aim the nozzle and squeeze.' "

She stood and headed to the door. "Those bees won't have a chance against me. I'll stand back and hose them down."

"And kill all of them?" Charlie said.

Amy paused. "That's horrible. But if they're killer bees and attacking the old man, what choice do I have?"

"Well—" Charlie began.

Too late. She was out the door.

Charlie glanced at the computer screen, and a second later he jumped from his chair and dashed out the door after Amy.

At the sight of Amy, the man stopped honking. It was oddly silent, because none of the bees were flying. They were stuck in a huge mass on the rear window of the car. Not even buzzing.

Amy held the nozzle in front of her and walked slowly toward the car.

"Do you know the range on that?" Charlie asked.

"I'll figure it out when I get there," she answered. "I'll get as close as I can, and as soon as they swarm toward me, I'll blast them."

"They won't swarm you," Charlie said.

"Look, they're attacking the man in his car!"

"No. They're not. Follow me, okay? And don't do anything to them unless they start to fly toward us."

Charlie was nervous enough to give the car a lot of room as he walked around the hood to get to the other side. He glanced behind him. Amy followed him, aiming the fire extinguisher nozzle in the direction of the bees.

So far, so good.

As they went around the front of the car, Charlie glanced at the man inside. He had leaned forward and was holding the steering wheel with both hands. Charlie saw that a beagle was in the front seat, on his rear legs and looking into the back seat at the window full of bees. And barking.

Charlie gave the man a thumbs-up. And hoped what he had just googled was accurate.

When Charlie and Amy reached the other side of the car, the man cracked down his window. A little.

"I stopped just down the road to let my dog out for a walk," the man whispered. "We got back in, and the bees swarmed! Driving down the road didn't shake them loose from the car. I saw your sign and thought a vet would know what to do."

He gave a weak smile. "The fire extinguisher is a good idea."

"I know, right?" Amy said.

"A better idea is to open the back door on this side," Charlie said.

"What? And let the bees in? If they sting my dog, he'll probably die!"

"No," Charlie said. "To let one bee out. The queen bee."

"Queen bee?" the man said.

"I think that's what's making your dog bark."

Charlie peered into the back seat. "And I see her there. Crawling along a seat belt. She's huge."

Amy looked too.

"Charlie," she said. "How did you know that?"

"I asked my friend Google," he said. "It just took three words. **Bee. Swarm. Car.**"

"The swarm is protecting the queen bee?"

"Yup," Charlie said. "It happens a lot. A dozen stories popped up right away. The queen bee must have gotten stuck in the vehicle when you stopped to let your dog out. So all we need to do now is get the queen bee out of the car, and things will be just fine."

"Okay," Amy said. "And after that, how about we tell the man stuck in the bathroom that his cat will be just fine too."

"Maybe not if it's a tumor," Charlie said.

Amy grinned. "How about you ask your friend Google if cats have belly buttons?"

Chapter Three

The next morning, Charlie and Amy walked through some light rain on the way to the clinic.

Charlie stopped in the parking lot and pointed to the ground at something he had placed there the night before. "Seriously?"

"Gross," Amy said. "Somebody didn't pick up after their dog."

"Looks like something else," Charlie said. He picked it up. "Cigar. Toss it in a can. It is so tragic."

He tried to hand it to Amy.

"That's okay." She gave him a fake sweet smile. "I don't want a soggy cigar that looks like something else. I'll let you toss it in the trash."

Charlie shrugged. It looked like his plan had worked.

Amy opened the door to the clinic, and Charlie followed her inside, still holding the soggy cigar.

On the other side of the waiting room, a woman sat with a chocolate Labrador in front of her on a leash. In another chair, as far away as possible, a second woman held a Chihuahua on her lap.

Charlie walked toward the counter to drop the cigar in the garbage can.

"Good morning!" Amy said brightly to the women. "Nice to see you both.

Did either of you happen to notice that poster? The one about walking dogs? I'm trying to earn money to buy my mother a birthday present."

"So sweet," the woman with the chocolate Lab said. "I'll keep you in mind for Flagger here."

"I think I'll hire you," said the woman with the Chihuahua. "But my little Weezy here is a sensitive dog, and you'll have to help him in a special way."

Weezy started barking.

"Hush, puppy, hush!" the woman said. Weezy kept barking. She reached into her pocket and gave him a treat. He stopped.

"No problem!" Amy said. "Thanks! What's your name?"

"Mrs. Richardson."

"Thanks, Mrs. Richardson."

"I'm Miss Redding," the other woman said. "I've got Flagger here because he swallowed a necklace."

"Oof," Amy said. "We're going to need rubber gloves."

When she met Charlie behind the counter, he said, "You didn't even ask what Mrs. Richardson needed that was special."

"Whatever it is, it won't be a problem," Amy said. "You know me. I figure things out when I need to."

"Like attacking innocent bees with a fire extinguisher?"

"Win some, lose some," Amy said. "Things change all the time anyway, so why not just learn how to go with the flow? It's way less stressful."

"There's a good reason to follow rules," Charlie said. He always had a notebook in his back pocket so he could write down new rules he had learned. "They help you make sure as little as possible is unexpected. Like rule 53."

Rule 53:
It's easier to control bigger dogs than smaller dogs.

"Show me," Amy said.

He handed her his notebook.

She flipped the pages and then read rule 53 out loud: "*It's easier to control bigger dogs than smaller dogs.*"

"Nice try," Amy said, handing him back his notebook. "How about write down rule 82. 'It's not that easy to fool Amy Ma.' You want me to help your mom with the big dog because we might need to flush out that necklace with food that has a lot of fiber in it, right?"

Charlie knew that dogs often swallowed small objects. If those objects had sharp edges, the veterinarian would suggest surgery to remove them, to make sure they didn't cut the dogs' insides. But Miss Redding had described the necklace as smooth. Charlie guessed his mom would decide it was safer for Flagger not to have surgery and to let the necklace come out more naturally.

Charlie told Amy. "You're right about that. Probably no surgery. Lots of fiber. And an overnight stay to make sure he's fine."

"And the little dog?" Amy asked.

Charlie looked at a clipboard. "Weezy needs a stomach operation."

"See? Rule 82. You can't fool me. You're just trying to put me in charge of helping your mom with the big dog so you can have the easy job with the little dog."

"No," Charlie said. "There's a good reason for rule 53. There's always a good reason for a rule."

"Sure, sure, my sneaky friend," Amy said with a grin. "If that's so true, then why don't I take Weezy in when your mom is ready for him."

"If anything goes wrong, don't say I didn't warn you," Charlie said.

He pulled out a piece of paper, set it on the counter and wrote something on it.

"In the meantime," Charlie said, "read this. I put the cigar in the parking lot last night and made sure this morning that we walked to the clinic together."

CIGAR. TOSS IT IN A CAN. IT IS SO TRAGIC.

Amy understood immediately.

"Good one!" She grinned and gave Charlie a high five. "Like I said. Win some, lose some. I lost that one. But you already lost the next; have fun with Flagger and waiting for the jewelry to flush out. Don't forget your gloves!"

Chapter Four

Down the hall, a woman in a tracksuit pushed open an exam-room door. She held a pet carrier with a black cat inside. Charlie's mom, Selena, walked into the hallway after her.

She spoke to the woman. "Give Zooloo a few days and she'll be her usual spry self."

The woman nodded and smiled. She and Selena walked together down the hallway to the waiting room.

"Weezy is next," Charlie told Amy.

Amy stepped over to take Weezy from the woman in the chair.

Just as Amy picked up Weezy, the woman with the cat stepped into the waiting room.

Weezy saw Zooloo in the pet carrier and jumped out of Amy's arms. He scrambled across the floor and leapt at the woman, causing her to drop the carrier.

The door of the carrier popped open, and Zooloo jumped out and ran under a chair beside Flagger.

Flagger looked down at the cat and yawned.

Charlie scooted out from behind the counter and scrambled for Zooloo under the chair.

"Weezy!" Amy shouted.

Weezy barked louder and dashed toward the cat.

"Weezy!" Mrs. Richardson called. "Hush, puppy, hush!" she cooed.

Charlie managed to reach the chair just before Weezy did.

Zooloo hissed at Charlie from her hiding place.

Charlie tried to scoop up the cat, but she slashed out with a paw, drawing lines of blood across Charlie's hand. Charlie yelped and backed away.

Weezy rushed past Charlie's ankles in a brown blur, yapping and snarling.

Zooloo scampered beneath the next chair. Then the next chair. But Weezy was so small, he followed easily, the claws of his tiny feet scratching along the clinic floor. Weezy easily flushed the cat out from the safety of the chairs.

Zooloo ran along the wall with Weezy right behind her, snapping at her tail.

"Weezy!" Amy shouted, chasing after the dog.

"Oh no! Hush, puppy, hush!" Mrs. Richardson shouted.

Charlie was spinning in a circle in the middle of the waiting room, trying to follow the action.

The cat ran toward Charlie, then jumped high, climbing Charlie's body as if he were a tree.

Claws sank into his thighs. Then his belly.

Charlie cried out again.

The cat made it to the top of Charlie's head and sank her claws into his scalp. Charlie tried to pull her loose, but Zooloo hung on even tighter.

Weezy snapped at Charlie's ankles and then tried to scratch his way upward as well.

Amy attempted to grab the dog, but
he snapped at her arm, and she pulled
away just in time.

"Let's all find a calm place," Selena
said. She stood directly over Weezy and
reached straight down. She placed her
hands beneath his belly and lifted him
up. His paws wriggled uselessly against
air. He turned his head to try to snap
at Selena, but her hands were secure

around his ribs, and he couldn't reach her with his furious jaws.

"Why don't you slowly step back to the wall," Selena said, looking at Charlie and the cat on his head. "Give Zooloo a chance to relax."

Charlie took a few steps backward. The cat dug in harder with her claws to keep from falling as he moved. Charlie gritted his teeth.

"Poor Zooloo," the woman said in a soothing voice. "Poor Zooloo."

She gently pulled the cat loose from Charlie's head, cradled her to her chest and kissed the top of Zooloo's head. "Mommy will give you a treat when we get to the van."

Poor Zooloo? Charlie looked at his hand and the lines of blood from Zooloo's claws. He wondered what his scalp looked like. *How about poor Charlie?*

"I'm so sorry, everyone," Amy said.

"Amy," Selena said. "Please don't feel bad. Small dogs are sometimes difficult to control because we are afraid of hurting them by holding them too tightly. Especially a Chihuahua."

As she spoke, Weezy wriggled in midair. "I've found this grip is the only way you can be sure to hang on to such a small dog," Selena said. "Charlie learned this the hard way too. Right, Charlie?"

Charlie nodded. Rule 53.

"Well, everyone," Selena said, "glad things are back to normal. Amy, Miss Redding has assured us that the necklace has smooth edges, so how about you take care of Flagger. And Charlie, why don't you follow me and Weezy to the back. Looks like you're going to need some disinfectant and bandages before we get Weezy taken care of."

As much as Charlie felt little stabs of pain, he wasn't too upset. After all, now Amy had the unfortunate job of finding the jewelry that Flagger had swallowed.

Chapter Five

"Got that king trapped yet?" Charlie's dad, Finley, asked. He was a very tall man who almost always wore a cowboy hat, cowboy boots, jeans and a hoodie. "We're at the park."

"Almost." Charlie didn't look up from his device. He sat in the passenger side of the pickup truck. They had gone into town to get groceries. On the way in, they had dropped Amy off at Mrs. Richardson's house so that she could take Weezy for a walk.

"I don't see Amy," Finley said. "This is where we were supposed to meet her, right?"

Charlie finally looked up. He was in the middle of a chess game. One of the things Charlie liked about chess was that you had rules to follow, and you could only win by using those rules.

The park was a grassy square in the middle of town. It had lots of large trees, benches and walking paths.

"Amy did say to find her here," Charlie said, letting his eyes scan the open areas between the trees. "Just look for a Chihuahua wearing one of those white cones and—"

He blinked. Was he seeing what he thought he was seeing?

"Oh boy," Finley said. "There's the little dog with a white cone. Please tell me that's not Amy beside him."

On the far side of the park, Weezy was on a leash, trotting proudly even though the white cone looked bigger than Weezy himself.

The face of the person holding the leash was not visible. Because the person walking Weezy was wearing a matching white cone on their shoulders.

Charlie remembered what Mrs. Richardson had said to Amy in the waiting area. *My little Weezy here is a sensitive dog, and you'll have to help him in a special way.*

"Oh boy is right," Charlie said. "I'm pretty sure that's Amy." He laughed. "I bet she thinks this is hilarious. I need a photo."

"Maybe not," Finley said. "I think what you should do is send her a text and tell her we are running a little late. Tell her to meet us at Mrs. Richardson's house."

"But we aren't late," Charlie said.

"We will be after I run back to the grocery store. Trust me on this."

Charlie laughed again. "Then I guess you don't know Amy like I do. She'll love a photo of this."

"You know I usually give you advice only when you ask for it, right? So when you don't ask and I give you advice, that should tell you something."

Charlie barely heard his father. He was already pushing open the door of the truck. He hopped out, jogged across the parking lot and then across the grass.

"Amy!" he called out. "Amy!"

The cone on her shoulder must have blocked her hearing, because she turned Weezy and walked away from Charlie at a very fast pace.

Charlie ran to catch up.

"Amy!"

She stopped.

"Go away," she said. Her voice was muffled by the cone.

"We're here to take you and Weezy back."

"Go away!"

"And miss a chance at a great photo?"

Charlie aimed his phone.

She whirled around to face him. "Don't you dare!"

Too late. He snapped a photo of her with her mouth wide open and her face framed perfectly by the white cone.

And then Amy began to cry.

Chapter Six

Just after the clinic opened on Wednesday morning, a short woman with short hair came in and approached the counter, where Charlie sat near the phone. She had a large glass bowl in both hands and a worried look on her face.

"Hello," she said. "What's your name?"

"Charlie," he answered. "I assist Dr. Dembinksi."

"Hello, I'm Lizzie Stanton. Call me Lizzie. And this is Jenny."

Lizzie set the bowl on the counter. The bottom third of the bowl was filled with dirt and small twigs and stems of dried grass. In the center of the dirt was a huge tarantula. It was on its back, with all of its legs flat. It was not moving. It seemed like it was wearing a loose blanket of skin, with legs sticking out from the wrinkled skin.

"Are you afraid of spiders?" she asked Charlie.

"Not dead ones," he said.

"Jenny isn't dead," she told him. "I looked it up on the internet. If Jenny were on her stomach with her legs curled up beneath her, you would know she was dead. But Jenny is on her back. So are you afraid of live spiders?"

"Not ones in a glass bowl that don't move and look dead," Charlie said.

"Well, I'm terrified of spiders," she said. "I'm taking care of it for my daughter, Olivia, while she's on vacation. It looks like Jenny is stuck in the middle of molting. If this spider dies, it won't break my heart, but it will break Olivia's. Since I'm very afraid to touch it, I thought maybe Dr. Dembinski could help me."

"Dr. Dembinski has been called out to help a farmer with a horse. She'll be back in about an hour and a half."

"Oh no. The forums on the internet all agree it's important to help Jenny get unstuck as soon as possible."

"Jenny? Unstuck?" Amy had just walked into the waiting area from the back of the clinic. She was wearing rubber gloves. Charlie was glad to see that her gloves were clean.

Amy looked into the bowl. She jumped back and screamed.

She took a deep breath. "Sorry! Hairy death machines do that to me."

Amy leaned in over the bowl, took a closer look and shuddered. "Even dead hairy death machines."

"It's not dead," Charlie said. He pulled his notebook out of his back pocket and began to write. *Rule 88. Tarantulas on their stomachs with their legs curled beneath them and not moving are DEAD. Tarantulas on their backs and not moving may still be alive and trying to get out of their skin.*

That was the thing about Charlie's rules. You never knew when you might need one.

"But it may be dead soon," Lizzie said. "I'm Lizzie. What's your name?"

"Amy Ma. No *h* in Ma." Amy looked closer at the tarantula. "Charlie, while you're writing, maybe you should add this to your rule. 'Step on no pets.'"

That made sense to Charlie when it came to tarantulas that didn't move. He wrote, *Step on no pets.*

"Since you're already wearing gloves," Lizzie said to Amy, "maybe you can help with Jenny? I printed out instructions from the internet. All we need is a cotton swab. You keep it moist and use it to gently work the skin off the spider."

"These gloves are for a chocolate Lab who swallowed some jewelry," Amy said. "We're giving the dog lots of fiber and keeping him in a kennel until the jewelry comes out. I've already been through a couple of big piles since yesterday. I'm hoping I will find it in the next pile. Other than that, you probably don't want the rest of the details."

Lizzie made a face. "I agree. Enough said. Charlie, you're a vet's assistant.

Since Dr. Dembinski isn't here, perhaps you can help the spider molt."

"I'm not sure I should," Charlie said. What if he made a mistake with the skin, and the tarantula died? It would be his fault.

"I came here expecting to pay the vet," Lizzie said. "How about I give you the money instead?"

Charlie shook his head. He liked to have more time to plan, to think through a problem, before making any kind of decision.

Amy took a deep, deep breath. "I've got the gloves on anyway, and it would be horrible if the tarantula died, right? I guess you could pay me, if you like. I *am* trying to earn money for my mom's birthday present."

Lizzie smiled. "Thanks!"

Amy smiled back. "By the way, Charlie, would you mind showing Lizzie what you just wrote?"

He flipped open his notebook. Lizzie looked at the sentence. *Step on no pets.*

Amy said, "I wonder if that sentence is spelled the same forward as backward? You know, like my name."

"Huh," Lizzie said after thinking about it. "That's fun."

Charlie just groaned.

Chapter Seven

"Will it help if I apologize again?" Charlie asked Amy.

They were on their bicycles, riding in town, passing houses on a tree-lined street. They were almost at Miss Redding's house. It had taken them the usual twenty minutes to ride down the quiet road from the ranch into town.

"Huh? Apologize? Why do you think I'm mad at you?"

Charlie didn't want to tell her the reasons. First of all, Amy had not ridden her bike right beside his. She usually did that so she could look at him while they talked. Even though it was much safer to ride in single file, which was one of Charlie's rules.

Amy always argued that as soon as she heard a car on the road, she would either drop back or move forward. Her point was that once you understood a rule, you knew when you could safely ignore it. When there were no cars, it didn't matter where they rode their bikes. They could even ride in the middle of the road.

The second reason was that she hadn't talked nonstop like she usually did.

Charlie didn't want to mention this reason either. She might think he missed all the talking.

The third reason was that Amy had not challenged him to their usual race down the last stretch of the road into town. And he sure didn't want her to think he liked racing her, even though he always lost.

"Yesterday afternoon, when I took the photo of you in the park wearing a dog cone, I didn't do it to hurt your feelings. I really am sorry," Charlie said.

"I'm the one who is sorry. I'm sorry I cried and made you feel bad. You didn't know that lots of people had already taken photos, and I was getting more and more upset each time. Anyway, it only proved you were right. When Mrs. Richardson said I'd have to help her dog in a *special way*, I should have asked for more details. I didn't know she thought Weezy would need a human to wear a cone so he didn't feel silly wearing one."

This didn't help Charlie at all. If Amy wasn't mad at him right now, what else could be wrong?

Unfortunately, he didn't have time to ask her, as they had just reached Miss Redding's house. She was sitting on the front porch. She waved at them.

Amy pushed open the gate, and Charlie followed her up the sidewalk.

"Good news, Miss Redding," Amy said. "Here it is."

Amy held up the shiny, clean necklace she had pulled from her pocket. Charlie tried not to think about where it had been and how glad he was that he hadn't had to clean the necklace, rubber gloves or not.

"And Flagger is doing just fine," Amy said. "Dr. Dembinski wants to keep him till the end of day to make sure the necklace didn't cause any damage as it passed through. Have you lost any other jewelry?"

"That's a great question," Charlie said. "We don't want to have anything else sharp in Flagger's stomach, right?"

"Nothing else," Miss Redding said. "And you can bet I'll keep things safely out of Flagger's reach. I think he gets into mischief just to get my attention, especially when my boyfriend is around."

Miss Redding sighed. "But that doesn't seem like it's going to be an issue now, so I guess I have nothing to worry about! Unless you can also fix things with my boyfriend?"

Charlie wanted to turn around and leave. He couldn't think of a single rule in his notebook that would help in a conversation like this. Except maybe a new rule. *Never ask Charlie for advice about relationships.* Just look at what had happened the day before at the park, when he'd ignored his dad's advice to stay in the truck and leave Amy alone.

It seemed, though, that people liked talking to Amy about their problems.

"Your boyfriend?" Amy said, going to sit beside Miss Redding. "What happened?"

"That's just it," Miss Redding said, throwing her hands up. "I have no idea. It wasn't too long ago that he was talking about getting married. And now he doesn't seem interested at all." She patted Amy on the knee. "But that's something I'll need to figure out myself. You were so nice to ask though."

Chapter Eight

In the waiting room of the clinic, Charlie sat behind the counter as usual. He was sorting out letters to put on the sign out front. It was much easier to put up the new pun of the week when he got organized in advance. He sighed. He thought the new pun was really bad: **Why are frogs so happy? They eat what bugs them.**

On the other side of the waiting room, Amy and Mr. Leonard stood in front of a large Saint Bernard.

Mr. Leonard was an elderly man with round glasses and a wonderful smile. He held a toothbrush in one hand.

"Dr. Dembinski says you only need to worry about the front teeth," Amy said. "And that you shouldn't brush for longer than two minutes. Make sure you give Muggles a reward after."

"That sounds easy," Mr. Leonard said. "This looks like a regular toothbrush."

"It is," Amy said. "We keep a supply here just for this purpose. When you get home, make sure you don't get it mixed up with your own toothbrush!"

Mr. Leonard laughed with Amy. "I'll head home now with Muggles. Thank you, Amy. You're so much fun."

As he closed the door behind him, Amy was still smiling.

Charlie had finished sorting out the letters, and there was no one else in the waiting room. Normally he'd be happy to either play chess on his phone or read a science book. But his mom was encouraging him to think about other people and practice making conversation. She had suggested he try it with Amy, since Amy was such a good friend.

"Hey," Charlie said. "I hear your mom is getting married. Ha-ha."

Amy squinted. "Married?"

"Just joking," Charlie said. He thought if you added *ha-ha*, people would know it was joke.

"I don't get it," Amy said.

"At breakfast this morning, Mom was telling me and Dad about the ring she saw on your mom's hand. The one

you gave her for her birthday. I was so surprised. I didn't think you had saved up so much so soon!"

Amy said, "Well, sometimes there are other ways to get a ring. Just saying."

Charlie didn't give that comment much thought before he continued talking. "Either way, Mom said she joked with your mom about how real it looked. Then my mom asked your mom if she was getting married."

By the look on Amy's face, Charlie knew he had said something wrong. Maybe it was because Amy wished her own mom and dad were still married?

"Married?" she asked.

Charlie wished he hadn't begun this conversation. "You know, like it was an engagement ring instead of a fake diamond ring. Ha-ha?"

Amy's frown deepened.

Charlie was relieved when the clinic door opened and two young boys walked in. Both had bright red hair. The older one was Charlie's age and held a pigeon gently in his hands. The pigeon blinked and made cooing sounds. The younger boy looked about six years old and was crying.

"Hi," the older one said. "My mom is waiting out in the car. She said we need to bring this to you. We found him on the ground in our yard."

"He wasn't moving," the little boy said. "We saved him. He's ours. I named him Sleepy. I want to keep him."

"My mom says he belongs to someone else," the older boy said. He stepped closer and held the pigeon up. "Look at his legs."

There was a yellow band around each leg. Both bands were printed with black numbers.

Finally! A problem Charlie could solve!

"Hang on," Charlie said. At the computer, he googled *pigeon leg band.*

The answer came up immediately.

"It's a racing pigeon," Charlie explained, feeling proud. He scanned the article. "What's probably happened is that he flew too far and he's tired. All we need to do is give him water and grain and call the owners. They can decide if they want to come and pick him up. Or if they want him to fly back home after he's rested."

"But he's mine," the little boy said, crying louder. "Sleepy is my friend."

"You need to be brave, Joey," the older boy said. "We both know returning him is the right thing to do."

The older brother looked at Charlie. "That's why our mom sent us in by ourselves. She wants us to learn to be responsible and honest. The owner of the pigeon wouldn't want us to keep him."

"You can leave him with us," Charlie said. "We'll take good care of him. And we'll make sure to contact the owner. It looks like the band has all the information we need."

The older boy reached out to hand the pigeon to Amy. She took him and held him against her chest.

"No!" Joey cried.

His older brother hugged him. "If you lost your pet, wouldn't you want someone to call you?"

Joey hugged him back but said nothing. The older boy took him by the hand, and they went back outside.

As the door closed, Charlie said to Amy, "This should be some fun detective work, right? And he was right—the owner will be happy to hear from us."

Amy carefully handed Charlie the pigeon. "You do it. I'm going for a walk."

"A walk? But—"

"Not everybody can be lucky like you, Charlie," Amy said. "Not everyone has the perfect life and can follow all the rules and never make a mistake. Not everybody can build a perfect doghouse like you when they need money. Some people have to touch tarantulas even when they are terrified of spiders."

She slammed the door behind her as she walked out of the clinic.

Charlie blinked a few times. What had just happened? What had he done wrong?

The pigeon blinked back at him. And cooed again.

Charlie sighed and went back to the counter with the bird.

Chapter Nine

"We missed the turn to Mrs. Richardson's house," Charlie called to Amy from his bike, pointing down the street to the right.

"No," Amy said. "We have another stop to make first."

"Where?" Charlie asked.

"You'll find out soon enough. By the way, you're not good at keeping secrets. I saw what you have in the bag. The straw cowboy hats."

"It's the only reason you won the race," Charlie said. He had a large bag strapped to his back. "The bag kept flapping."

"Then explain the hundred other times you lost." She flashed him a smile. "And after that, explain why you brought along three cowboy hats."

Charlie was glad to see that Amy was feeling happier.

On this trip into town to Mrs. Richardson's house, she had ridden beside him and talked almost the whole time. *And* she had raced with him on the last stretch of country road. But she hadn't said a word about why she had been so angry the day before and stomped out of the clinic.

Charlie was curious about that. But not curious enough to start another conversation where he had no idea what was going on.

"It's a nice day," Charlie said.

"You're changing the subject. Why three straw cowboy hats?"

"I'd be happy to tell you after you tell me why we're making a stop along the way."

"I messed up," Amy said. "Now I need to make it right. That's all I'm going to say for now."

Charlie knew better than to try to make Amy talk. He followed her down the street, single file, of course. The sun was warm, and the breeze felt good.

Five minutes later she stopped at a building that had a sign across the front—**BOB'S PLUMBING AND HEATING.**

She leaned her bike across the side of the building, so Charlie did the same with his.

"What's up?" he asked.

"What's up with the cowboy hats?" she answered.

"I'll let you know when we get to Mrs. Richardson's to take Weezy for a walk."

"Fine. I need to get this over with anyway."

She took a determined step to the main door. Since she hadn't told him not to follow, Charlie stayed right behind her.

Inside, a man was at the counter. He was tall, with blond hair, and seemed younger than Charlie's dad.

"Bob?" Amy said.

The man nodded.

"I have something I think you lost," Amy said. She reached into her pocket, pulled something out and set it on the counter. A ring.

"What?!" He picked it up and examined it. It glittered in the sunshine that streamed through the front window. "It's—"

"An engagement ring?" Amy asked.

"How did you...where did you...?"

"Remember how Miss Redding lost her necklace?"

"I didn't know she had lost a necklace," Bob said. "She and I haven't talked for a few days."

"You mean since the night the ring disappeared?"

"Well, I had it out to polish it—I wanted it to be as shiny as possible when

I proposed. I left the room, and when I came back it was gone. I thought she'd seen it and hidden it so that I couldn't propose to her. I was hurt and afraid to ask her reason for hiding it, so I thought I'd take some time to think about what to do."

"She lost a necklace that night. I found it too. Let's just say it involved rubber gloves and waiting for her dog to move the necklace and ring through his system."

Wait, Charlie thought. Amy had also found a ring?

"Flagger swallowed it?"

"I found both the necklace and ring in the same pile."

Bob winced.

"Don't worry. I cleaned it. I also asked Miss Redding if she'd lost anything else. Since she hadn't, I wondered if Flagger had found it somewhere on a walk. I called the police station to see if anyone had reported a lost ring, and I looked at the newspaper ads. But nobody had reported anything." Amy was talking really fast now. "So I told myself it was probably one of those fake diamond rings, and I kept it. Then I found out it was an engagement ring, and I remembered Miss Redding saying that the two of you had ended your relationship even though she'd thought you were going to propose. So I thought it might be better to bring you the ring in case you really still wanted to propose to her. I mean, she would be way sadder knowing you had a ring and never gave it to her. And—"

"She thinks that I broke up with her?" Bob said. "I'm such an idiot. Hey, don't take this wrong, and thanks so much, but I have to run!"

Chapter Ten

Ten minutes later, Charlie and Amy reached Mrs. Richardson's house. It was a large brick house with a long driveway that led to a three-car garage.

Amy set her bike down flat on the ground, its front wheel still spinning. "Tell me about the hats."

Charlie carefully made sure his kick-stand was ready and set his bike upright. He pulled the bag off his back where he'd strapped it, pulled out the three straw cowboy hats and set them on the ground.

He also pulled out an orange, a potato and a pair of scissors and set them on the ground.

He tipped the bag upside down and shook it.

"Huh," he said. "How strange."

"Strange?" Amy echoed.

"No lemon. No melon."

"Why would you need a lemon and a melon to go with an orange, a potato and a pair of scissors? And here I thought *I* was the weird one."

"I can show you why I need the scissors." Charlie cut the top off one of

the hats, leaving a big circular hole. He put the circular piece of straw back in the bag.

"That doesn't explain anything," Amy said, her hands on her hips.

"Wear this," Charlie said, giving her one of the two good straw hats.

"That still doesn't tell me anything." But she slapped the hat on her head.

Charlie put the third hat on his own head and held the cut-out hat in his right hand. He walked up the driveway.

"Charlie!" Amy said. "What is going on?"

Charlie didn't answer. With all the times she'd driven him crazy, he was happy for the chance to keep *her* guessing.

Before he could even ring the doorbell, Weezy started barking up a frenzy on the other side of the door. Only a few seconds after that, Mrs. Richardson opened it. She was wearing a cone on her head.

Weezy kept barking from inside the cone around his face.

"Oh! Hush, puppy, hush!" Mrs. Richardson murmured.

Weezy continued barking until Mrs. Richardson gave him a treat. It wasn't Charlie's business, but it seemed like Weezy had figured out a really good way of getting treats.

"I didn't know there were going to be two of you," Mrs. Richardson said with a frown. "Weezy is sensitive, you know. He's going to feel ridiculous out in public unless both of you are wearing cones, but I only have one extra. This one."

She pulled it off her shoulders. "So who is going to take him for a walk, and who is going to stay behind?"

"Would you mind if I tried something?" Charlie asked. "I think my idea will make Weezy feel really good about going out in public. Especially since he is so *sensitive*."

"You can try. But if Weezy doesn't like it, then only one of you can go for a walk with him."

Charlie reached down and carefully undid Weezy's cone.

"Wait!" Mrs. Richardson cried. "He needs the cone so he doesn't bother his stitches."

Charlie grinned. He showed Mrs. Richardson the hat with a hole at the top. He slipped it over Weezy's head. The brim was wider than the cone had been.

"He can't reach the stitches now," Charlie said.

Mrs. Richardson clapped her hands in glee. "He looks delightful!"

"I've got a little bandanna for him too." Charlie pulled a red kerchief out of his pocket.

"Oh, let me!" Mrs. Richardson tied it around Weezy's shoulders. "My little cowboy!"

"When we get back, I can leave you the cowboy hats," Charlie said.

"So I don't look silly wearing a cone?" Mrs. Richardson asked as she handed Charlie the end of the leash.

Charlie, wisely, didn't answer. He was proud of himself for that. Maybe he was getting better at thinking about other people's feelings.

"Let's go, Weezy," Charlie said.

As they reached the end of the driveway, Amy said, "You're a really good friend. I feel bad for being so mad at you."

"I did take that photo of you yesterday when I didn't understand you were upset. I get that."

"No. It's about what I said yesterday. About you having the perfect life. Some days I'm just angry that my mom and dad aren't together. It's not your fault. And I was angry that I couldn't get my mom a great birthday present, because sometimes she's sad too. We're not a family with a lot of money."

"Well—"

"Don't talk, Charlie. Just listen. You always seem to know what's right or wrong. Sometimes I wish I had a set of rules to help me. I never should have kept the ring, and I knew it. I could have asked my mom what to do, but I wanted to surprise her."

"Well—"

"Don't talk, Charlie. Just listen. Rules are great. How's this for a rule? 'If it's not yours, don't keep it.' Turns out being honest with my mom was awesome. She said she had wondered how I managed to buy a ring that nice. When I guessed it might be Miss Redding's engagement ring and told my mom I had to return it because I didn't want to be dishonest, she said she was so proud of me that it was the best birthday present for her."

"Well..." Charlie waited for her to tell him to just listen.

"Okay, Charlie, now you can talk. And I'll listen."

"No lemon," he said. "No melon."

"I just poured out my heart to you, and all you can tell me is that you forget to put a melon and a lemon in the bag?"

"No *h* in Ma." He grinned. Victory was his. "No lemon. No melon."

She thought about it and grinned back. "Good one, Charlie."

Author's Note

I hope you enjoyed the story as much as I enjoyed learning about life in a veterinary clinic before I began writing it. The situations that Amy and Charlie face in *Hush, Puppy* are all based on true stories. If you ever become a veterinarian someday, who knows what kind of fun true stories you'll be able to share about the animals that you help!

Sigmund Brouwer is the award-winning author of over 100 books for young readers, with close to four million books in print. He has won the Christy Book of the Year and an Arthur Ellis Award, as well as being nominated for two TD Canadian Children's Literature Awards and the Red Maple Award. He is the author of the Charlie's Rules series, the Justine McKeen series and the Howling Timberwolves series in the Orca Echoes line. For years, Sigmund has captivated students with his Rock & Roll Literacy Show and Story Ninja program during his school visits, reaching up to eighty thousand students per year. Sigmund lives in Red Deer, Alberta.

The Politics of Simple Living

A New Direction for Liberalism

by
Charles Siegel

Preservation

aut
facere
scribenda

aut
scribere
legenda

Institute

ISBN: 978-0-9788728-2-3

Contents